www.mascotbooks.com

For more information, please contact:
Mascot Books
560 Herndon Parkway #120
Herndon, VA 20170
info@mascotbooks.com

CPSIA Code: PRT0312A
ISBN: 1-936319-32-2
ISBN-13: 978-1-936319-32-9

Printed in the United States

BRICK'S WAY
GO GREEN!

D'Brickashaw Ferguson

Illustrated by Sean Tate & Henry Wilson

"I would like to dedicate this book to God and my family, Kirsten, Mom, Dad, and my brother. Thank you for all that you do."

~D'Brickashaw Ferguson

"Yes, we won the game!" said David, stretching his arms up in the air as if to signal a touchdown. David and his friends, Miguel, Nicole, and Crystal were New York fans, and they knew that this victory meant the next game was for the league championship.

"What a performance by New York," said the TV announcer as the camera captured the excitement on the faces of the screaming crowd. "And how sweet this victory must be for offensive lineman, D'Brickashaw Ferguson, a native of nearby Freeport, New York. As it turns out, D'Brickashaw will be back in Freeport tomorrow supporting his high school team as they compete for the Long Island Championship."

"What? Brick is from Freeport?" said Miguel.

"Guys, he's coming back to our neighborhood! Let's see if we can meet him…and maybe even get an autograph!" said an excited David.

The kids arrived to the game just as D'Brickashaw was walking down to the field. "Good luck in the championship game, Mr. Ferguson," said David. "Thank you," said the local football hero.

The kids enjoyed getting to know D'Brickashaw, and they were especially thrilled to find out that he attended the same elementary school as them—Giblyn Elementary School. David gave D'Brickashaw an update about the school and informed him that the annual science fair was coming up soon.

David explained, "You see, we were assigned science fair subjects, and all the good subjects—like volcanic explosions—went to other groups. We got stuck with 'Creating a Green School.'"

"And the worst part is that the science fair is next week and we haven't even started!" exclaimed Crystal.

"Guys, I think you have a great topic. Sure you won't have explosions, but just think, you can come up with a plan and actually implement it to make your school—our school—better!" said D'Brickashaw. "Man…I wish I could help you guys, but I have my championship game on the same day as the science fair."

"We really wish you could help us too…" said David.

At that very moment, something strange happened! Bright lights appeared, sounds of electric currents could be heard, and D'Brickashaw's body began to shrink! When the lights finally stopped, D'Brickashaw was transformed into "Lil' Brick."

"Sooo cool!" said David. "Now you can help us with our school project!"

The next morning, Lil' Brick showed up at
school and went straight up to his new friends.
Just as they entered the school, they ran into
a couple students.

"Our science fair project will be awesome!
We're creating a volcanic eruption…and my
mom is a scientist, so she'll be helping us!"
said a boy. "Your group has no chance, ha ha!"

"Don't let them bother you," said Lil' Brick.
"Let's show them what teamwork is all about!"

They went straight to the library and found books about the environment and ways to conserve energy. Not only were the kids enjoying their time with each other, they were also learning many interesting facts that could be used in their science project.

The group came up with several simple ways the school could conserve energy. Next, it was on to the teacher's office to present their findings.

"These are great ideas, gang!" Mr. Brown said, excitedly. "You have my permission to put your plan into action!"

With the "Giblyn Green Plan" approved, it was time to get to work. In one classroom, Lil' Brick and Crystal put up signs telling students to turn off the lights when they left the room. Miguel and David made sure all computer screens were set to sleep mode when they were not being used. Nicole and Crystal set up paper recycling stations in each classroom.

In the cafeteria, special bins were set up for paper, plastic, and aluminum items. Lil' Brick and Nicole talked to the school janitors about the importance of using environmentally friendly cleaning supplies. Their plan was coming together nicely!

Finally, it was the day of the Giblyn Elementary School Science Fair. The judges started to walk around, and their first stop was the volcanic eruption science project.

"Three…two…one…eruption!" said a student, and with that, lava began to flow out of the volcano. But something went wrong, sending the fake red lava all over the room! The spray landed all over their presentation materials, and even on the judge's head! It was a disaster! Everyone shared a laugh.

With Lil' Brick's help, his friends completed their science fair project. Not only did they have an informative presentation, their plan to create the "Giblyn Green School" was something the school community could embrace for years to come. For their efforts, the group received a blue first place ribbon!

At that moment, Lil' Brick realized that he needed to transform back to D'Brickashaw because he had to play in the championship game! David then went over near Lil' Brick and said, "I wish D'Brickashaw would become big again, so he can play in the big game!"

And soon after, a rainbow of lights swirled around him. Before Lil' Brick knew it, he was back to his grown-up size.

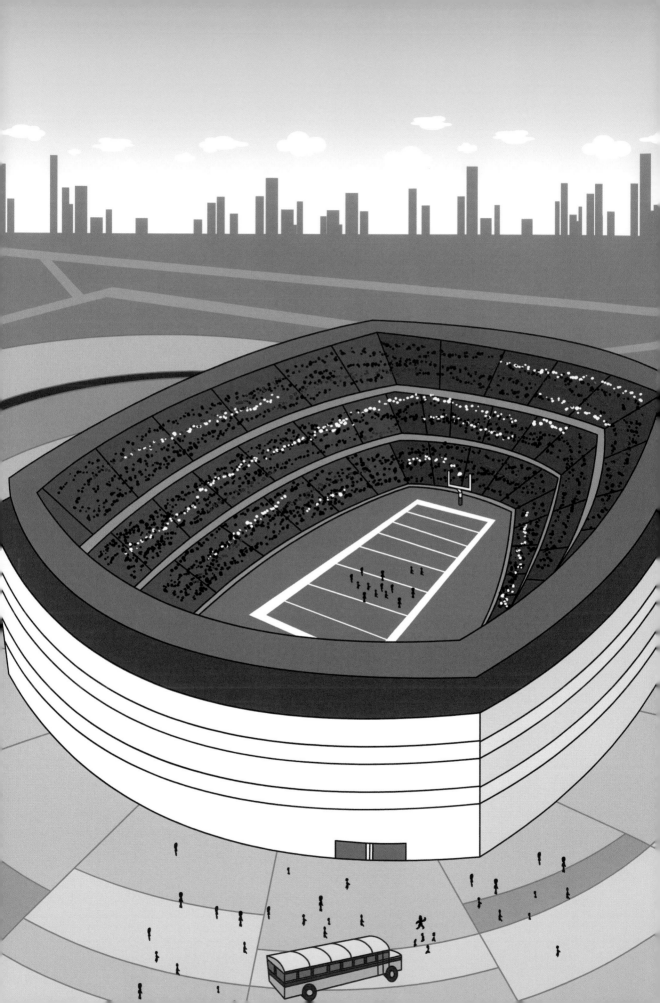

D'Brickashaw and his friends boarded a nearby school bus and asked the driver to take them to the football stadium...fast!

Finally, the bus arrived at the stadium! D'Brickashaw changed into his football uniform and ran onto the field just moments before the start of the game.

D'Brickashaw and his teammates played a great game and won the championship! He celebrated on the field with the team where he answered questions from reporters.

"Congratulations, D'Brickashaw! Why do you think you played so well today?" asked a reporter.

Turning to his friends, D'Brickashaw said with a wink, "I had some extra help from another green team!"

About Brick

D'Brickashaw Montgomery Ferguson was born on December 10th, 1983, to Rhunette and Edwin Ferguson Sr. Raised in Freeport, a suburb in Nassau County; D'Brickashaw would attend Freeport High School where he would realize his passion for football. D'Brickashaw chose to attend the University of Virginia in 2002. A four year starter, he would make his mark on the college football landscape. D'Brickashaw would set many records at Virginia, including one for the most starts by a freshman with 14 starts. He would also beat Ray Robert's long-standing record for most starts by offensive linemen, starting 49 consecutive games. D'Brickashaw would go on to become an All-American as well as gain All-ACC 1st team honors throughout his tenure, all while earning a B.A. in Religious Studies. The New York Jets selected D'Brickashaw Ferguson with their first pick (4th overall) in the 2006 NFL draft. D'Brickashaw would pick up where he left off, earning All-NFL rookie honors his first year in the NFL. D'Brickashaw is a 3-time NFL Pro Bowler and has started every game during his time with the New York Jets, a mark few can claim.

D'Brickashaw loves to give back to his community. In 2007, he founded the D'Brickashaw Ferguson Foundation. An organization devoted to offering scholarships to deserving students and the granting of assistance to food banks, clothing ministries, and funding repairs to existing churches. D'Brickashaw is the face of the New York Jets' new campaign "Eat Right, Move More", where he goes from school to school advising children on the necessity of healthy eating habits and being more active. D'Brickashaw has also given his time to assist with such events as the Special Olympics, the Lupus Walk, Autism and Muscular Dystrophy charities, The Covenant House, and the Athletes In Action organization. In May of 2009, United Way honored D'Brickashaw with recognition for his foundational work and his community efforts. In 2010, Freeport named a street after him and it now stands as D'Brickashaw Ferguson Way. This street was also the origin of the title of this book. Currently, D'Brickashaw Ferguson is a part of United Way's Team NFL, an initiative that hopes to recruit one million volunteer readers, tutors, and mentors in order to combat America's high school dropout rate. D'Brickashaw Ferguson is married to Kirsten Ferguson and they currently reside in New Jersey.

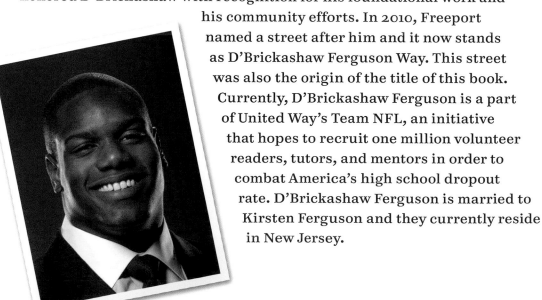

THE D'BRICKASHAW FERGUSON FOUNDATION

Building Communities...One Brick at a Time!

The mission of the D'Brickashaw Ferguson foundation is to improve the quality of life for students by awarding academic scholarships to those deserving; eligible students who reside in the New York area, including but not limited to Baldwin, Freeport, Hempstead, Roosevelt, Uniondale communities, and to other eligible students throughout the United States. The foundation will provide resources that will enhance and contribute to each student's pursuit of higher education. The foundation also provides financial support to churches by way of grants for the repair and construction of church owned edifices and provides resources to churches, schools, and to fund clothing and food ministries in hopes of building up the respective communities, thereby showing God's love in action.

For more information on The D'Brickashaw Ferguson Foundation please visit:

www.dbrickashawfergusonfoundation.org